PETER
AND THE
TIMBER WOLF

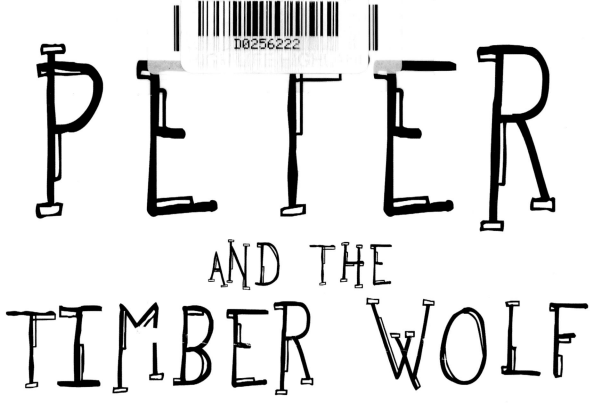

Written by
ANN BRYANT
Illustrated by Joseph Witchall

Peter and the Timber Wolf

"Hello!" says Peter. "Hello world!" And he opens up the gate.
This is a day for adventure, and Peter cannot wait!

The forest is hiding behind the field. It's deep and dark in there.
But this is the day of the brightest sun. There's magic in the air.

For Kidenza

A wonderful organisation, who with their professional musicians, bring classical music in fun-form to thousands of children.

To find out more about Kidenza visit their website:

www.kidenza.co.uk

Published by Caboodle Books
Illustrations by Joseph Witchall
ISBN 978-0-9954885-2-6

"Hello!" says Peter. "Hello world!" And he opens up the gate. This is a day for adventure, and Peter cannot wait!

The forest is hiding behind the field. It's deep and dark in there. But this is the day of the brightest sun. There's magic in the air.

"Morning, Peter! Morning Peter!" sings Bertie the Bird on high.

"I can look down on the world up here… I'll tweet you from the sky!"

"So what do you see, my feathered friend?" calls Peter from down below.

"Just field and forest," Bertie replies, "and clouds that come and go!"

Peter grins and goes on his way for a day that's packed with fun,
A day for exploring and making camps, the day of the brightest sun.

And then there appears a fat white Duck poddling and waddling by
And Bertie the Bird says not a word, but Peter and Duck say hi.

And suddenly all is silent.

Even the grass is still.

Even the basking butterflies and the sheep that graze on the hill.

And the leaves on the trees hardly move in the breeze.

It's totally calm until…

…the Bird and the Duck pick a pointless fight with a beak and a quacking bill.

It's Bertie who starts the argument with, "Lazy old Duck
needs sacking!"
And the Duck in a flap runs forward then back,
angrily quacking and quacking.

Bertie says, "Swimming is easy-peasy,
just going round and around."
And Duck replies, "Swimming is cooler by
far than hopping along on the ground."

And that makes Bertie really cross. "I'm not just a hopper, I also fly!"

And Duck says, "Really? Do you? Hmm? Well, now that you mention it, so do I!"

And arguing on and on like this, they don't see Cat come creeping by.

And Cat thinks great, a nice little bird, too busy by far to notice me.

Creepety creep, I'm ready to pounce, before he can fly to the tree.

"Watch out!" Peter shouts. "Watch out Bertie Bird! Watch out! There's a cat over there!"

And Bertie goes whoosh with a beat of his wings, and soars up high in the air.

Meanwhile the Duck swims around and around,
cautiously eyeing the Cat.
And Cat with a purr starts preening her fur. "I actually
much prefer rat!"

Then out of the house comes Grandma. She's wearing a face like thunder.

"Peter, a Wolf might come out of the woods! And who'd be his lunch, I wonder?"

Huh! thinks Peter, there's no way a Wolf would stray out here in the sun.

He turns to his Gran. "You said I could play! You said that today would be fun!"

"Forget it!" says Grandma, striding off, "Come now, before it's too late.

We can go to the park, we can go out for tea, but first I'm locking the gate!"

As Peter turns to follow his Gran, he can't believe what he sees.

A Timber Wolf comes out from the trees, and the world all around seems to freeze.

There's a beating of wings and a scratching of claws and the Cat scrambles up in the tree.

And out of the pond jumps the terrified Duck, as afraid as a Duck can be.

And she waddles and poddles and tries to escape but the legs are not long on a Duck.
And she's losing her lead as the Wolf gathers speed, thinking, "Duck! What a great piece of luck!"

And Peter and Birdie and Cat watch in horror as Wolf cries, "Yummy yum yum!"
And swallows the Duck in a great big gulp from his mouth straight down to his tum.

So Bertie is perched on a branch of the tree.
On another, the cool Cat lies.

While Wolf stalks around and around the tree, staring up with his big greedy eyes.

And this is the setting, this is the scene, full of twitters, meows and sighs,

Now Peter's thoughts are bubbling away after all that he's seen and heard.

An idea is racing around in his head about saving the Cat and the Bird.

And all the way home, as he follows his Gran, he works on his plan, full of hope.

Peter's determined to catch the Wolf. He just needs a very strong rope.

In no time at all he's back with the rope and climbing the old stone wall,

Then he spreads out his arms and shakily walks, taking care not to slip or fall.

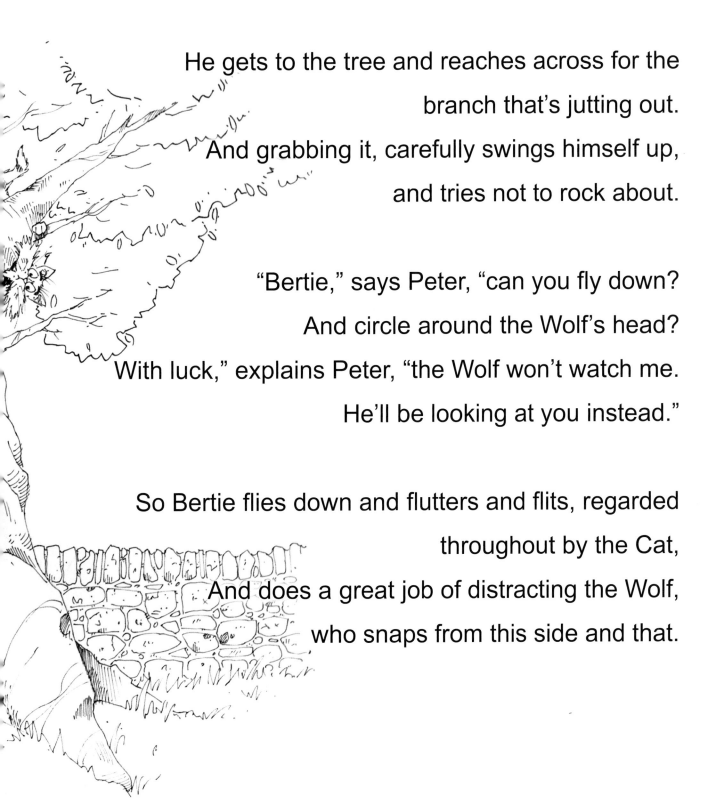

He gets to the tree and reaches across for the
branch that's jutting out.
And grabbing it, carefully swings himself up,
and tries not to rock about.

"Bertie," says Peter, "can you fly down?
And circle around the Wolf's head?
With luck," explains Peter, "the Wolf won't watch me.
He'll be looking at you instead."

So Bertie flies down and flutters and flits, regarded
throughout by the Cat,
And does a great job of distracting the Wolf,
who snaps from this side and that.

And Peter starts talking under his breath.

"Mister Wolf, this is for you!"

As down goes the rope, but it's not just
a rope.

It is now the perfect lasso!

And the Bird is so close that the Wolf thinks yes!

I can swallow him all in a bite.

But Peter has managed to catch the Wolf and is tugging
with all his might.

How the Wolf jumps, how the Wolf leaps, all the time pulling
the noose.

But tied to the tree, the rope becomes tighter, the more the
Wolf tries to break loose.

At that very moment some Hunters appear, looking from left to right.

But Peter calls loudly,...

"Wolf can't escape. **Don't shoot!**

He's tied up tight!"

Now, the Hunters, and Bertie and Peter and Cat, know exactly what to do.

They form a triumphant procession, and off they go to the zoo.

Peter is first, Cat is next, though she keeps trying to get ahead.

Then it's the Hunters leading the Wolf, then
Grandma, her cheeks all red.
"I knew that a wolf would come out of the woods.
I knew it! Remember, I said?"

Above them flies Bertie, tweeting away… *En route.*
About to arrive.
Who caught the wolf? WE caught the wolf! Yo
Peter! Thumbs up! High Five!

And now, listen carefully. Can you hear this? It's the Duck. She was swallowed… **ALIVE!**

About the author

Ann Bryant

Ann Bryant is the internationally published author of about 120 books, largely children's fiction, including the three very popular series Ballerina Dreams, School Friends and Families in a Step-Chain. Ann also writes music resources for primary schools, such as the award winning Teaching KS1 Music.

Trained at the Royal College of Music, Ann taught music for over twenty five years, specialising in EYFS and KS1, as well as writing for numerous BBC school programmes.

She wrote the theme and incidental music for a series of thirteen pre-school children's programmes for the BBC called Tales of Aesop. When she's not writing, Ann travels in the UK and abroad giving 'author' talks in schools, and leading music education workshops for teachers.

She is the Patron of Reading for the primary schools in the Bailiwick of Guernsey and is currently writing music curriculum for pre-schools in India.

Peter and the Timber Wolf brings together the two sides of Ann's career. Ann says "Integrating the arts, especially words and music, is my passion."

To find out more about Ann, visit her website:
www.annbryant.co.uk